William and the Prize Cat and Other Stories

Richmal Crompton, who wrote the original *Just William* stories, was born in Lancashire in 1890. The first story about William Brown appeared in *Home* magazine in 1919, and the first collection of William stories was published in book form three years later. In all, thirty-eight William books were published, the last one in 1970, after Richmal Crompton's death.

Martin Jarvis, who has adapted the stories in this book for younger readers, first discovered *Just William* when he was nine years old. He made his first adaptation of a William story for BBC radio in 1973 and since then his broadcast readings have become classics in their own right. BBC Worldwide have released nearly a hundred William stories on audio cassette and for these international best-sellers Martin has received a Gold Disc and the British Talkies Award. An award-winning actor, Martin has also appeared in numerous stage plays, television series and films.

Titles in the *Meet Just William* series

William's Birthday and Other Stories
William and the Hidden Treasure and Other Stories
William's Wonderful Plan and Other Stories
William and the Prize Cat and Other Stories
William and the Haunted House and Other Stories
William's Day Off and Other Stories
William and the White Elephants and Other Stories
William and the School Report and Other Stories
William's Midnight Adventure and Other Stories
William's Busy Day and Other Stories

All *Meet Just William* titles can be ordered at
your local bookshop or are available by post
from Bookpost (tel: 01624 836000).

William and the Prize Cat and Other Stories

Adapted from Richmal Crompton's
original stories by Martin Jarvis

Illustrated by Tony Ross

MACMILLAN CHILDREN'S BOOKS

First published 1999 by Macmillan Children's Books
a division of Macmillan Publishers Limited
20 New Wharf Road, London N1 9RR
Basingstoke and Oxford
www.panmacmillan.com

Associated companies throughout the world

ISBN 0 330 39098 8

7 9 8 6

A CIP catalogue record for this book is available from
the British Library.

Typeset by SX Composing DTP, Rayleigh, Essex
Printed and bound in Great Britain by Mackays of Chatham plc, Kent

Contents

William and the Prize Cat 1

William's April Fool's Day 21

William and the Twins 39

Revenge is Sweet 61

Dear Reader

Ullo. I'm William Brown. Spect you've heard of me an' my dog Jumble cause we're jolly famous on account of all the adventures wot me an' my friends the Outlaws have.

Me an' the Outlaws try an' avoid our fam'lies cause they don' unnerstan' us. Specially my big brother Robert an' my rotten sister Ethel. She's awful. An' my parents are really <u>hartless</u>. Y'know, my father stops my pocket-money for no reason at all, an' my mother never lets me keep pet rats or <u>anythin'</u>.

It's jolly hard bein' an Outlaw an' havin' adventures when no one unnerstan's you, I can tell you.

You can read all about me, if you like, in this excitin' an' speshul new collexion of all my fav'rite stories. I hope you have a jolly gud time readin' 'em.

Yours truly

William Brown

William and the Prize Cat

William and Ginger ambled slowly down the lane. Henry and Douglas had succumbed to a local epidemic of mumps, and so William and Ginger were the only two representatives of the Outlaws at large.

Suddenly, round a bend in the roadway, they ran into the Hubert Laneites, their rivals and enemies from time immemorial.

Hubert Lane, standing in the centre of his little band, smiled fatly at them.

"Hello," he said. "Been to the circus?"

Hubert Lane had a knack of finding out most things about his enemies, and he was well aware that the Outlaws had *not* been to the circus, because they had not enough money for their entrance fee.

"Circus?" said William carelessly. "Oh, what circus?"

"Why, the one over at Little Marleigh," said Hubert, slightly deflated.

"Oh, *that* one," said William, smiling. "Oh, you mean that one. It's not much of a circus, is it?"

Hubert Lane had recourse to heavy sarcasm.

"Oh no. It takes a much grander circus than that to satisfy you, I suppose."

"Well," said William mysteriously, "I know a jolly sight more about circuses then *most* people."

The Hubert Laneites laughed mockingly.

"How do you know more about circuses then most people?" challenged Hubert.

William considered this in silence for a moment, then said, still more mysteriously, "Wouldn't you like to know?"

Hubert eyed him uncertainly. He suspected that William's deep mysteriousness was bluff, and yet he was half impressed by it.

"All right," he said. "You prove it. I'll believe it when you prove it."

"All right," retorted William. "You jolly well wait and see."

Hubert sniggered, but for the present he turned to another subject.

"I'm getting up a cat show this afternoon," he said innocently. "There's a big box of

chocolates for the prize. Would you like to bring your cat along?"

The brazen shamelessness of this for a minute took away William's breath.

It was well known that Hubert's mother possessed a cat of gigantic proportions which had won many prizes at shows.

That the Hubert Laneites should try to win public prestige for themselves and secure their own box of chocolates by organising a cat show, was a piece of impudence worthy of them.

"Like to enter your cat?" repeated Hubert carelessly.

William thought of the scrawny creature which represented the sole feline staff of his household.

Hubert thought of it too.

"I suppose it wouldn't have much of a chance," said Hubert at last, with nauseating pity in his voice.

"It would. It's a jolly fine cat," said William indignantly.

"Want to enter it then?" said Hubert, satisfied with the cunning that had made William thus court public humiliation.

The Browns' cat was the worst-looking cat in the village.

"All right," he said. "I'll put you down. Bring it along this afternoon."

William and Ginger walked dejectedly away.

Early that afternoon they set off, William carefully carrying the Browns' cat, brushed till it was in a state bordering on madness, and adorned with a blue bow taken off a boudoir cap of his sister, Ethel, at which it tore furiously in the intervals of scratching William.

"Well, it's got spirit anyway," said William proudly. "And that ought to count. It's got more spirit then that fat ole thing of Hubert's mother's."

As if to corroborate his statement the cat shot out a paw and gave him a scratch from forehead to chin, then leapt from his arms and fled down the road still tearing madly at its blue bow.

"There," said Ginger. "Now you've gone and done it. Now we've got to go without a cat or not go at all."

William considered these alternatives gloomily. "Mmm. An' they'll go on and on, 'cause they know we can't go to the circus," he added.

"Well, what shall we do?" said Ginger.

"Let's sit down and wait a bit," said William, "and try 'n' think of a plan. We might find a stray cat bigger 'n theirs. Let's just sit down and think."

Ginger shook his head at William's optimism.

They were sitting down on the roadside, their backs to the wood that bordered the road. William turned to look into the wood.

"There's wild cats anyway," he said. "I bet there's still a few wild cats left in England. I bet *they're* bigger than his mother's ole cat. I shun't be a bit surprised if there were some wild cats left in this wood. I'm goin' to have a look anyway."

And he was just going to make his way through the hedge, when the most amazing thing happened.

Out of the wood, gambolling playfully, came a gigantic – was it a cat? It was certainly near enough to a cat to be called a cat. But it was far from wild.

It greeted Ginger and William affectionately, rolling over on to its back and offering
itself to be stroked and rubbed.

They stared at it in amazement.

"It's a wild cat," said William. "A tame
wild cat. P'raps hunger made it tame. P'raps
it's the last wild cat left in England. Puss! Puss!
Puss!"

It leapt upon him affectionately.

"It's a *jolly* fine wild cat," he said, stroking
it, "and we're jolly lucky to have found a cat
like this. Look at it. It knows it belongs to us
now."

"We'd better take it to the show," said
Ginger. "It's nearly time."

So they made a collar for it by tying
Ginger's tie loosely round its neck, and a lead
by taking a bootlace out of William's boot and
attaching it to the tie, and set off towards the
Lanes' house.

The other competitors were all there,
holding more or less unwilling exhibits, and
in the place of honour was Hubert Lane

holding his mother's enormous tabby.

But the Lane tabby was a kitten compared with William's wild cat.

The assembled competitors stared at it speechlessly as William, with a nonchalant air, took his seat with it, amongst them.

"That – that's not a cat," gasped Hubert Lane.

William had with difficulty gathered his exhibit upon his knee. He challenged them round its head.

"What is it then?" he said.

They had no answer. It was certainly more like a cat than anything.

"'Course it's a cat," said William, pursuing his advantage.

"Well, whose is it then?" said Hubert indignantly. "I bet it's not yours."

"It *is* mine," said William.

"Well, why have we never seen it before then?" said Hubert.

"D'you think," said William, "do you think we'd let a valubul cat like this run about all over the place? Let me tell you, this is a 'specially famous cat, that never comes out except to go to shows, and that's won prizes all over the world. Well, I've not got much time. I've gotter get back home. So if our cat's bigger 'n yours you'd better give me the prize now. This cat's not used to bein' kept hangin' about before bein' given its prize."

The Hubert Laneites sagged visibly gazing at the monster which sat calmly on William's knees, rubbing its face against his neck affectionately.

Hubert Lane knew when he had met defeat. He took the large box of chocolates on which the Hubert Laneites had meant to feast that afternoon and, still gaping at the prizewinner, handed it to William.

The other exhibitors cheered. William put the box of chocolates under his arm, and set off leading his exhibit.

It was not till they reached the gate that the Hubert Laneites recovered from their

stupefaction and yelled as with one accord, "Who can't afford to go the circus? *Yah*!"

William was still drunk with the pride of possession.

"It's a jolly fine wild cat," he said again.

"Where'll we keep it?" said Ginger practically.

"In the old barn," said William, "an' we'll not tell anyone about it. We'll keep it there an' take it out for walks in the wood an' bring it food from home to eat. Then I vote we send it in for some real cat shows. I bet it'll win a lot of money. I bet it'll make us millionaires. An' when I'm a millionaire I'm going to buy a circus with every sort of animal in the world in it."

The mention of the circus rather depressed them. And Ginger, to cheer them up, suggested eating the chocolates.

They descended into the ditch and sat there with the prize cat between them.

It seemed that the prize cat, too, liked chocolates and the three of them shared them equally till the box was finished.

"Well it's had its tea now," said Ginger, "so let's take it straight to the old barn for the night."

"You don't know that it's had enough," said William. "It might want a bit of something else. We'll take it to the old barn, then you go home and get some food for it."

"All right," said Ginger. "I'll bring it what I can find with no one catchin' me. It'll depend whether the larder window's open."

Ginger departed and William amused himself by playing with his prize cat. It was an excellent playfellow.

It made little feints and darts at William. It rolled over on the ground. It growled and pretended to fight him. The time passed on wings until Ginger returned.

Ginger's arms were full. Evidently the larder window *had* been open.

He was carrying two buns, half an apple pie and a piece of cheese, and yet despite this rich haul his expression was one of deepest melancholy.

He placed the things absently down upon a packing case and said, "I met a boy in the road, and he'd just met a man, and he said they were looking for a lion cub that had got away from the circus."

William's face dropped. They both gazed thoughtfully at the prize cat.

"I – I sort of thought it was a lion cub all the time," said William

"So did I," said Ginger hastily.

13

After a long silence, William said, "Well, I suppose we've gotter take it back."

He spoke as one whose world had crashed about him. Life without the lion cub stretched grey and dark before him, hardly worth living.

"I s'pose we've gotter," said Ginger. "I s'pose it's stealin' if we don't. Now that we know."

They placed the food before the cub and watched it with melancholy tenderness.

It ate the buns, sat on the apple pie, and played football with the piece of cheese.

Then they took up the end of William's bootlace again and set off sorrowfully with it to Little Marleigh.

The proprietor of the circus received the truant with relief and complimented the rescuers on its prompt return.

They gazed at it sadly, Ginger replacing his tie, and William his bootlace.

"He's a cute little piece, isn't he?" said the

proprietor. "Don't appear yet. Too young. But goin' to lap up tricks like milk soon. Well I'd better be getting a move on. Early show's jus' goin' to begin. Thank you, young sirs."

"I s'pose," said William wistfully, "I s'pose we couldn't *do* anything in the show?"

The proprietor scratched his head.

"I tell you what. I am short-handed as it happens. I could do with another hand. Just movin' things off an' on between turns. Care to help with that?"

So deep was their emotion, that William broke his bootlace and Ginger nearly throttled himself with his tie.

"I should – jolly well – think – we would," said William.

The Hubert Laneites sat together in the front row. They'd all been to the circus earlier in the week, but they'd come again for this last performance partly in order to be able to tell the Outlaws that they'd been twice, and partly to comfort themselves for the fiasco of their cat show.

"I say," said Hubert Lane to Bertie Franks, "I say, won't old William be mad when we tell him we've been again."

"Yeah," said Bertie Franks. "Yeah. And I say, fancy him havin' the cheek to say he knew more about circuses than us and not even been once. We won't half rag him about it. We won't . . ."

His voice died away. He stared down into the ring. For there unmistakably was William, setting out the little tubs on which the performing ponies performed.

He rubbed his eyes and looked again. It *was* William.

"*Golly*," he said faintly.

All the Hubert Laneites were staring at William, paralysed with amazement.

"*Golly*," they echoed and drew another deep breath as Ginger appeared carrying the chairs on which the clown pretended to do acrobatic feats.

Then the circus began. The Hubert Laneites did not see the circus at all. They were staring fascinated at the opening of the tent into which William and Ginger had vanished.

After the first turn they emerged and moved away the little tubs and brought out a lot of letters, which they laid on the ground for the talking horse to spell from.

After that turn, William came out alone and held a hoop for Nellie the Wonder Dog to jump through.

Not once did the expressions of stupefied amazement fade from the faces of the Hubert Laneites.

The next day they approached William with something of reverence in their expressions.

"I say, William," Hubert said humbly. "Tell us about it, will you?"

"About what?" said William.

"About you helpin' at the circus."

"Oh, *that*," said William carelessly. "Oh I gen'rally help at circuses round about here. I don't always go into the ring, like what I did yesterday, but I'm gen'rally in the tent behind helpin' with the animals, trainin' 'em for their tricks, getting 'em ready and such like. I said I knew a jolly sight more about circuses than what you did, you remember?"

"Yes," said Hubert Lane still more humbly. "It must be jolly fun, isn't it, William?"

"Oh, it's all right," said William. "It's hard

18

work, and of course it's jolly dangerous. Trainin' the animals and lockin' 'em up for the night and such like."

He walked a few hundred yards with an ostentatious limp, and then said, "The elephant trod on my foot yesterday when I was puttin' it in its cage."

He touched the scratch that his mother's cat had made.

"The bear gave me this the other night, when I was combin' it out ready to go on and do its tricks. It's work not everyone would like to do."

They gazed at him as at a being from another and a higher sphere.

"I say, William," said Bertie Franks. "If – er – if – they want anyone else to help you, you'll give us a chance, won't you?"

"I don't s'pose they will," said William. "'Sides, this circus has gone now and I don't know when another's comin'. It's dangerous work, you know, but I'm used to it."

And, followed by their admiring eyes, he limped elaborately away. He was limping with the other foot this time. But of course, no one noticed that.

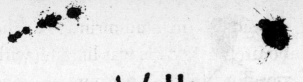

William's April Fool's Day

April the First was a day generally enjoyed to the full by William, but this year something seemed to have gone wrong.

Not one of his efforts had been successful.

Ethel had calmly put on one side, without even attempting to crack it, the empty eggshell that he had carefully arranged in her egg-cup.

Robert had removed the upturned tin-tack from his chair before sitting down, and had placed it so neatly upon William's that William had been taken unawares.

His father had refused even to raise his eyes from his newspaper at William's excited

21

shout, "Look, Father, there's a cow in the garden."

And his mother had merely murmured, "Yes, dear" when William had informed her that Ethel had been bitten by a mad dog on her way to the village.

His attempts to make April Fools of his Outlaws had been no more successful. They were all, indeed, so much upon their guard that none of them would answer the simplest question or pay heed to the most innocent remark.

At last, they abandoned hostilities and formed an offensive alliance against the other boys of the neighbourhood.

But not even this was successful. The other boys of the neighbourhood, also, were too well up in the rules of the game to be taken in by the well-worn tricks the Outlaws played on them.

Advised of the near approach of bulls, runaway horses, motor cars out of control, they merely made faces at the Outlaws.

Informed that sweets were being given away at Mr Moss's sweet shop, that a circus had just arrived at the other end of the village, that Farmer Jenks was riding round his farmyard on his old sow, they merely remarked, "Yah! April Fool yourself!"

"I wish we could find someone that had forgotten it was April Fool's Day," said Henry.

"Tell you what I'd like to do," said William dreamily. "I'd like to make someone really important an April Fool. Let's think who's the most important person living here."

"The Vicar?" suggested Ginger.

"The doctor?" suggested Douglas.

"Yes, I think the doctor," said William. "He'd be easier to make one, anyway . . . I know! I've thought of something to bring them *both* in."

Followed by his Outlaws, William made his way up to the doctor's front door, knocked at it smartly and informed the maid who opened it that the Vicar was dying and would the doctor please go to him at once.

For answer he received a box on the ear that nearly made him lose his balance.

He rejoined his friends, rubbing his boxed ear tenderly and filled with righteous indignation.

"Huh! S'pose it was true an' they'd let the poor Vicar die. Well, I think she's the same as a murderer, that woman is. I've a good mind to go an' *tell* the Vicar that she's as good as murdered him. I bet I was as near dead as you could be too, with a bang like that on the side of my head. She oughter get put in prison for murdering both of us. I'm jolly well sick of April Fool's Day, anyway. I vote we go and play somewhere . . ."

It was decided that it would be hardly safe to play in their own village. Their own village was too full of their enemies, eager to use the noble festival of All Fools' Day as an opportunity of getting even with them.

They could not safely relax their guard for a moment in their own village.

"Let's go over to Marleigh," suggested Ginger, "an' take the football with us."

The Outlaws were comparatively unknown in Marleigh.

"Good," agreed William. "We'll get a bit of peace there."

They set off briskly across the fields to Marleigh and there found a vacant plot of land on which to hold a football match.

"A beastly house next to it, of course," said William morosely, "and they'll be sure to make a beastly fuss every time the ball goes into the garden. I don't think there's a single place left to play in England that hasn't got a house next to it, all ready to make a fuss the minute your ball goes into its garden. Sometimes I feel I don't care how soon the end of the world comes."

"Well, come on, let's begin to play," said Ginger.

They began to play and, in a few minutes, as William had prophesied, their ball went over the wall into the garden of the house.

It was a high brick wall with no convenient

foothold on it, so they went to the gate to survey the enemy's ground.

There they found that to get round to the side garden where their ball was, they would have to pass a window where a haughty-looking lady sat at a writing-table. Clearly it could not be done.

"We'll have to go to the door and ask," said William cheerfully. (William's spirits always rose at a crisis.) "I'll put on my polite look."

William's polite look, though much admired by himself and his friends, was in reality a sickly leer.

It certainly did not seem to ingratiate him with the housemaid who opened the door.

"Please can we go round to your garden to get our ball, if you don't mind, thank you very much?"

The housemaid stared at him disapprovingly, disappeared, and soon returned to say shortly, "She says it's an intolerable nuisance, but you can this once."

"Thank you very much," said William,

widening his leer and making her a courtly bow.

"None of your impudence!" she said, and slammed the door in his face.

The Outlaws went round to the side of the house and found the ball.

They returned to the plot of waste land and continued their interrupted match.

In five minutes the ball had gone over the wall again. They considered the situation with some dismay.

"I'm not going to ask again," said William firmly. "She'll start murdering me same as the other one did if I go. You'd better go, Ginger."

"All right," said Ginger and began to compose his features into an imitation of William's leer as he walked up to the front door.

The same housemaid opened it, received Ginger's dulcet request with obvious indignation, then retired to report it to her mistress.

She returned almost immediately.

"She says you ought to be ashamed of

yourselves pestering like this. She says you can get it this once, but she says she'll send for the police if it goes on."

Ginger retrieved the ball and rejoined his friends.

"Gosh!" he said. "More like dragons than yuman bein's round here, aren't they? We'll take jolly good care not to let it go over again, anyway."

They returned to their game but five minutes later an energetic and unguarded kick from Douglas sent the ball once more into the forbidden garden.

"Well, it's you or Henry to get it now," said William. "Me an' Ginger's had our turns."

"They all look pretty savage about here," said Douglas. "They look as if they'd kill you as soon as look at you. I votes we go home an' leave it."

"Yes, I dare say you do," said William. "It's not your football. It's my football, an' I'm not goin' home without it, so there!"

"What are you goin' to do then?"

"I'm goin' to get it. I'm goin' to crawl round to the garden on my hands and knees, so's she can't see me from the window, an' get it."

"I'll come with you," said Ginger.

"So will I," said Douglas and Henry.

There was no need for more than one to go to fetch the ball, but when there was any danger the Outlaws liked to face it together.

In single file, on hands and knees, they made their way to the garden and retrieved the ball.

In single file, on hands and knees, they began their journey back.

But, just as they were passing beneath the window, Ginger sneezed, and the amazed and indignant face of the lady of the house appeared in the window, disappeared, then reappeared now more indignant than amazed at the door.

The Outlaws rose sheepishly to their feet.

The lady stood barring their path and giving eloquent voice to her indignation.

"Disgraceful . . . *disgraceful*! I've a good mind to send for the police and have you charged for trespassing. If I ever see any of you inside this garden again, I'll send for the police at *once* . . . Go away this *minute*. If I knew who your parents were, I'd write to them most strongly."

The Outlaws fled, William clutching his beloved football.

"Well, it's time to go home, anyway," he said.

"Yes, it's nearly twelve," said Ginger,

pretending to consult his watch (which never went for more than five minutes) but in reality glancing at the church clock that showed above the trees.

"Nearly twelve," said William wistfully, "and we've not made anyone an April Fool. It'll be the first year I ever remember that we've not made anyone an April Fool."

"We've not been made one ourselves, anyway," Ginger reminded him.

"Huh – 'course not!" said William scornfully. "Catch anyone makin' April Fools of *us*! That's not the point. The point is that we've not made anyone one. It seems awful somehow not to have made anyone an April Fool on April Fool's Day."

"Well, it's not quite twelve yet," said Ginger. "It's not too late."

"Yes, but who is there to make one here?" said William.

At that moment a boy was seen coming towards them.

He was fat and pale, and he looked both

stupid and conceited. The Outlaws took an immediate dislike to him.

"Let's make *him* one," whispered William.

"Yes, but *how*?" said Ginger.

"I know!" said William.

The boy had come abreast of them now. He gave them a challenging grimace.

"I say," said William with well-assumed friendliness, "what do you like best? What sort of cakes, I mean?"

"Coconut buns," answered the boy promptly.

William gave a short surprised laugh.

"Well, that's a funny thing."

He pointed to the house that had been the scene of their escapade.

"You see that house?"

"Yes," said the boy.

"Well, the lady that lives there, she always gives coconut buns to any boys who come to ask if they can get their ball from her garden. If you want some coconut buns all you have to do is go up to the door and knock and ask

if you can speak to the mistress of the house. And when you get to her, all you've got to say is that you're one of the boys who've been playing ball just outside her garden this morning, and the ball's gone over again, and may you fetch it. And when you've said that, she'll give you some coconut buns."

The boy stared at them.

"Go on," William urged him, glancing at the clock, and seeing the fingers perilously near the fatal hour.

"Go on. We *want* you to have those buns 'cause – you look hungry. See here . . ." desperately he took a treasured whistle from his pocket, "I'll give you that if you'll go an' say it."

The boy took and pocketed it without a word.

William's urgency communicated itself to the others.

They felt that their very honour depended upon somehow or other making this boy an April Fool before twelve o'clock.

"And look here," said Ginger feverishly. "I'll give you this penknife, too, if you'll go quick. We – we *want* you to have those coconut buns."

The boy pocketed the penknife, too, stared at them for another moment, then said, "All right" and, walking up to the front door, rang the bell.

The housemaid opened it and he was admitted. The door closed. The Outlaws danced a silent dance of triumph and delight at the gate.

Then they waited impatiently for the fleeing form of their victim to issue, pursued by the wrath of the redoubtable lady of the house.

Nothing happened.

"Perhaps she's rung up the police," said William, looking anxiously down the road.

"Well, if she has, we've made April Fools of them," said Ginger triumphantly.

"I – I hope she's not murderin' him," said Douglas. "We shall get into a beastly row if we've got him murdered."

But at that moment an upstairs window was flung open, and the boy appeared at it.

He held a coconut bun in one hand, the whistle and penknife in the other.

He grinned and munched and waved his spoils at them exultantly.

"W-w-w-what are you doing there?" stammered William.

"I live here," shouted the boy. "It's my home. Yah-boo! April Fools!"

He laid down the coconut bun and took up a pea-shooter.

The clock from the church tower struck twelve.

"April Fools!" called the boy again.

The Outlaws turned and began to walk slowly down the road.

A pea caught William neatly just above one ear.

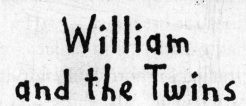

William
and the Twins

Honeysuckle Cottage stood empty and William (who took a great interest in Honeysuckle Cottage) always made a short detour on his way home from school in order to see if there were any signs of new inhabitants.

His joy therefore was great when, one evening, he saw unmistakable signs of occupation, all the windows open, and an easel standing in the little garden. An Artist.

Next morning he was up early and made his way to Honeysuckle Cottage. He crept cautiously up the path and peered in at the open kitchen door.

And there he stood motionless, for a most extraordinary couple were engaged upon preparations for breakfast.

Both had exactly the same face – pale and narrow, framed in short, lank, fair hair.

Both wore white silk shirts and coats of homespun tweeds.

That one was a man and the other a woman was evident from the fact that one wore knickerbockers and the other a skirt. Beneath these garments they wore worsted stockings and brogues.

Both were leaning over the gas stove, the man anxiously watching a saucepan of six eggs, the woman making coffee.

The woman turned round suddenly, and saw William standing in the open door-way.

"Watch this and see that it doesn't boil," she said to him casually, "or else take those plates into the dining-room."

"I'll take the plates," said William, thrilled at being thus accepted as a member of the party. He carried the plates into the dining-room. "These eggs are done, I should think."

"Have I done too many? I just put in all the man brought."

"Oh no," said William reassuringly. "I don't think they're too many."

The man seemed cheered. "No, I suppose there aren't."

The woman came in with the coffee, and he pointed to her, to William, and to himself.

"No, of course, just two each, isn't it? That's not too many."

William sat down. The woman passed him a cup of coffee, the man gave him two eggs, and the meal began. The strange couple accepted him without question.

Suddenly the woman looked at him and said, "Why aren't you drinking your coffee?"

"I never drink coffee," said William. "I don't like it."

She looked at the man and sighed. "He's right, you know," she said. "One shouldn't

drink stimulants of any sort if one wants to keep the psychic faculties unclouded."

She turned to William again. "What do you drink?"

"I drink liqu'rice water mostly," said William.

"Liquorice water," she said vaguely. "I must try it."

William, who had finished his eggs, murmured something about going home to breakfast.

He departed quietly homeward, where he made an excellent breakfast of porridge, scrambled eggs, toast, butter and marmalade.

After school he made his way at once to Honeysuckle Cottage.

The man was seated at an easel in the little orchard, and the woman in a deck-chair on the little lawn.

She looked at William and said, "Do you see nature spirits?"

William stared at her in amazement.

"Children often do see them," went on the lady, "though my great friend Elissa Freedom – you may have heard of her, she's well known in the psychic world – says that she didn't see them as a child, though she sees them now quite plainly. I really must show you some of her photographs. She has a lovely one of a birch tree with the outline of a nature spirit standing near it. About the size of a child . . . faint, you know, but quite unmistakable. She says that everything in nature has its attendant spirit. Of the same colour generally. I've brought a camera with me, but so far I haven't had any success."

"Uh-huh," agreed William, completely mystified.

"That, of course, is why Tristram and I have come here," she went on. "Tristram is my twin brother. We want to cultivate our psychic faculties. My brother will – er – surrender himself to psychic influences in the hope of doing inspirational painting, and I am going to try to cultivate my psychic vision till I can see a nature spirit. I take it that you are interested in the psychic side of life?"

"Uh-huh," agreed William again.

"Have you had any experiences?"

"Me?" said William. "Oh yes, lots."

But before he could tell her any of his favourite imaginary exploits, the church clock struck five, and she rose slowly from her deck-chair.

"It's tea-time, I suppose," she said. "Of course, one shouldn't really drink stimulants when one's trying to acquire psychic vision."

As they entered the kitchen, she turned suddenly to William.

"What did you say you drank?"

"Me?" said William. "Liqu'rice water mostly."

"Liquorice water? I don't think I've ever tasted it. Where do you get it?"

"I make it," said William modestly.

He pulled a bottle out of his pocket and with an air of great gallantry poured some into a saucer for her to drink.

She tasted it with a critical frown. The frown vanished.

"It's very nice," she said. "A pure herbal drink, of course."

"Uh-huh," said William.

"You must show me how to make it," she said.

William was thrilled. He'd never before met a grown-up who did not look upon liquorice water as a messy juvenile concoction to be thrown away whenever discovered.

Tristram came in from his easel in the

45

orchard. His sister poured him a saucer of the liquorice water.

"I thought, Tristram," she said, "that during this retirement from the world we should give up stimulants. They dull the psychic faculties, you know, so we're having liquorice water."

Tristram tasted it.

"Delicious," he said. "Quite delicious."

"The boy made it," said his sister, "but I dare say the stores could get it for us. The boy always drinks liquorice water and he says that he has had psychic experiences."

William had come to the conclusion that "psychic" was a synonym for "exciting".

The woman said, "Have you had any success, Tristram?"

"N-not exactly," he confessed. "I – surrender myself and try to paint what comes into my head, as it were, but I can't help realising that it isn't as good as the work in which I *don't* surrender myself . . ."

The activities of the sister (whose name, William had discovered, was Miss Auriole Mannister) were not *very* exciting.

She sat gazing wistfully about the little garden, her camera poised for action upon whatever nature spirit should appear to her.

She asked William to leave the garden undisturbed to her between four and five o'clock, explaining that she thought that her psychic functions were most active then.

But William was finding the artist in the orchard even more interesting than the vision-seeker in the garden.

The artist sat before his easel with a palette in his hand, executing on his canvas a series of amazing strokes that reminded William of the nightmare he had had after last year's November the Fifth's firework display.

The artist noticed William's expression and said in his gentle, melancholy voice, "It's not meant to represent what one sees, you know. It's meant to represent the emotions the sight of it rouses in one."

"Yes," said William, trying to sound as if he understood.

William hadn't realised that painting pictures – real pictures – was *quite* as easy as that, simply splodging paint about anyhow. It simplified the art considerably.

He surreptitiously tore pages out of his exercise books at school, and took them to the cottage with him.

There, he "borrowed" paint very cautiously, till he found that the artist took the situation as a matter of course.

If William happened to be using the paint

tube he wanted, he would wait quite patiently till William had finished with it.

Gradually, William came to look upon himself as an accomplished artist.

He boasted of his skill to his friends till Ginger said, "All right, paint us something then, an' let's see."

"All right, I will," said William. "What'll I paint you?"

"Paint us a sign to put up at the ole barn."

"All right. What'll I paint on it?"

"A lion."

William began his lion that evening. Tristram was working indoors in water colours. Both of them set to work, side by side.

Once, Miss Auriole looked in and whispered, "How are you getting on, Tristram?" and Tristram said, "I'm surrendering myself *utterly*, but I don't know what the results will be."

"I *do* hope it will be all right," said his sister, and added, "I'm waiting and watching with my camera outside."

William finished his lion. He considered it an excellent lion. It looked as spirited and ferocious as a lion ought to look.

He went outside to look at Miss Auriole. She was asleep in a deck-chair with her camera on her knee.

Then he went home and didn't realise till he was in bed that he'd left his lion behind in the little studio.

After school next day, William took Ginger

round to the cottage. They entered the garden cautiously, and crept towards the study window.

"My painting's in here," William said, then he stopped.

Through the study window he could see his two friends and a strange man with a beard standing round the little desk.

He retreated.

"We'll wait till they come out," he said.

"Let's have a game of Hide and Seek," said Ginger.

"All right. I'll hide. You count."

"One . . . two . . . three . . ."

William crept down to the bottom of the lawn where the heap of grass cuttings stood, and with a dexterous movement inserted himself into the very middle of it.

Soon he heard Ginger shout "Com—" and stop suddenly.

Then he heard the sounds of the lady setting up her deck-chair on the lawn.

William remained in his grass heap

wondering what to do. It was the hour during which the lady had asked him to leave her undisturbed.

For a moment he considered remaining where he was, till the end of the hour, but he was already tired of swallowing grass cuttings.

If he waited just a few minutes, it would be all right; she'd be fast asleep.

He waited till he imagined that he heard deep breathing, then rose from the heap, fled behind the greenhouse and out through a hole in the hedge.

Simultaneous sounds of a gasp and a click pursued him. Scattering grass cuttings at every step, he hastened down to the road.

He eventually found Ginger hanging about the gate of the cottage.

"Hello!" he greeted William. "I had to go 'cause she came out. Where were you hidin'?"

"In the grass."

"Well, let's try 'n' get your paintin' now."

They entered the little garden again.

Tristram was just joining his sister on the lawn.

"Tristram!" she greeted him excitedly. "I've seen one. Oh, my dear! It was so thrilling. I was sitting here as usual with my camera, watching and waiting, when suddenly, from that grass heap, there detached itself a faint green wraith – a shadowy spirit. For one second I saw it standing by the heap as plainly as I see you now, and then it disappeared."

"You got a snap of it, I hope," said Tristram anxiously.

"Yes, my dear. Oh, I hope so. If what I saw comes out, I can die happy. And what about your paintings, my dear?"

Tristram's face clouded over.

"It's no good. Tosher says that none of them will do for the journal. He says that they aren't *inspirational enough*."

"Oh, *Tristram*! I'm so sorry. Where is he? Has he gone?"

"No, he's still in the study. His train doesn't go till half-past."

"Let's go out for a walk, dear. It will do you good. He won't mind being left till his train goes, I'm sure."

Together the twins set off for their walk. Together Ginger and William crept round to the little studio, but the man with the beard was still there.

"I can't get it now," said William.

"I don't b'lieve you ever did it," said Ginger.

"All right," said William, "you wait till tomorrow."

Tomorrow came, and William went into the little studio, but he couldn't find his lion painting.

Ginger spent a pleasant day jeering at him, and then they both completely forgot the incident.

There were all the signs of departure at Honeysuckle Cottage. Boxes stood packed on the doorstep. The decrepit village taxi was at the little gate.

William hung about disconsolately. He was sorry to say goodbye to his friends. Suddenly he saw the postman at the gate, and he went down to get the letters.

There were two bulky packets – one for Tristram, and one for his sister.

Auriole fell upon hers with a cry of joy, and unwrapped half a dozen papers bearing the inscription *Psychic Realm*.

"My photograph!" she said, turning over

the pages with trembling fingers. Then she gave a scream of excitement.

"Here it is! Look!"

William and Tristram looked.

There was a photograph of the grass heap at the end of the lawn and, by it, the grass-covered figure of William, preparing to creep furtively away.

Beneath it was the legend: "Nature Spirit, photographed by Miss Auriole Mannister".

William gaped at it, speechless with amazement.

Before he could say anything, however, Tristram, too, had uttered a cry of surprise and excitement. He too had unwrapped half a dozen copies of *Psychic Realm* and had a letter in his hand.

"Listen," he said, "it's from Tosher. He says, 'After you'd gone I found a really splendid bit of inspirational painting in your studio. Why didn't you show it to me? It's truly inspired. I have called it *Vision* and it's reproduced on page 26.'"

Both of them turned over the pages frenziedly. "Here it is! Look!"

And there was William's lion, and underneath the words, "*Vision*: inspirational painting by Mr Tristram Mannister".

"But do you know," said Tristram in an awestruck voice, "I haven't the slightest memory of ever doing it."

"You must have done it in a state of ecstasy, dear," said Miss Auriole reverently.

"I must," said Tristram. "It's – it's the most wonderful thing that's ever happened to me."

Then the cab driver called to them saying that, blimey, they'd miss it if they didn't hurry, and they had gone before William recovered the power of speech.

They had, however, left a copy of *Psychic Realm* behind them, and William, with mingled feelings of pride and bewilderment, picked it up and put it in his pocket.

He showed the two pictures to everyone he knew, pointing out that the Nature Spirit

was himself, and that he had executed the inspirational painting of *Vision*.

No one, of course, believed him.

Revenge is Sweet

The Outlaws were agog with excitement, for the day of Hubert Lane's party was drawing near. This may sound as though the Outlaws were to be honoured guests at Hubert's party.

Far from it.

For between the Outlaws and the Hubert Laneites a deadly feud waged, and tradition demanded that they should treat each other's parties with indifference.

It was the Hubert Laneites who had broken that tradition. They had deliberately wrecked William's party the week before.

They had substituted a deceased cat for the

rabbit which the conjuror had brought with him and which was to appear miraculously from his hat.

The Outlaws were now out for revenge.

They were determined to wreck Hubert Lane's party, as Hubert Lane had wrecked theirs.

The news that Mr and Mrs Lane would be away for the party and that Hubert's Aunt Emmy would preside heartened the Outlaws considerably.

The Outlaws had met Aunt Emmy. Anything vaguer, kinder, more short-sighted, and more well-meaning than Aunt Emmy, could scarcely be imagined.

The Outlaws had made no definite plans. William, like all the best generals, preferred not to draw up his own plan of action till he had ascertained the enemy's.

The party was to begin at seven. At half-past six, ten boys in single file might have been observed creeping through a hole in the fence that bordered the Lane garden.

At the head crept William, his freckled face contorted into a scowl expressive of determination to do or die.

Behind him came Ginger, behind him Henry, behind him Douglas, and behind Douglas came six anti-Laneites and supporters of the Outlaws.

A pear tree grew conveniently up the side of the Lane mansion . . .

Hubert was in his bedroom at the other side of the house, anxiously arraying himself in an Eton suit and shining pumps.

The maids were in the kitchen giving the final touches to mountains of sandwiches and trifles and cakes and jellies and blancmanges.

Mr and Mrs Lane were away at the bedside of an exasperatingly healthy aged relative, and Aunt Emmy was in the kitchen driving the maids to distraction by her well-meant efforts to "help". She had already sprinkled salt over a trifle, under the impression that it was sugar.

So there was no one to oppose or even notice the Outlaws as, one by one, they climbed up the perilous branches of the pear tree and in at an attic window.

They sat on the floor and looked at each other, collars and ties awry, jackets torn, knees scratched and dirty.

The Lane attics consisted of three fair-sized rooms, packed with boxes, water cisterns, spiders' webs and mysterious pipes.

On the tiny landing outside was a small window leading straight out on to the roof. It was a boyhood's paradise.

The eyes of the Outlaws gleamed as they explored it. Then William called the attention of his band to the immediate object of the expedition.

"We've gotter creep out an' see what's happ'nin' first of all," he said hoarsely, "an' then – an' then we'll think what to do."

Very creakingly, on tiptoe, the Outlaws crept out after him and hung over the banisters of the attic staircase. Aunt Emmy's voice, clear and flute-like, arose from the hall.

"*That's* right, Hubert darling. You look *very* nice, my cherub, very nice indeed. *Quite* a little man."

"Your hair's coming down, Auntie," said Hubert.

"Little boys mustn't make personal remarks, darling," said Aunt Emmy.

The Outlaws were listening with silent rapture to this. William was storing up every word of the conversation in his mind for future use.

Then came the sound of the front door bell.

"The first guest, darling," said Aunt Emmy. "I'll open the door and you'd better stand just there to receive them – remember to say 'How d'you do?' nicely."

Then came the sound of the arrival of Bertie Franks, the most odious of the Hubert Laneites next to Hubert himself.

Arrivals followed fast and furious after that.

The Hubert Laneites all bore a curious physical resemblance to Hubert, their leader. They were all pale and fat.

They rallied round Hubert chiefly because of his unlimited pocket-money; and, like Hubert, when anyone annoyed them, they told their fathers and their fathers wrote notes about it to the fathers of those who had annoyed them.

The guests changed into pumps and drifted into the drawing-room. A dismal, very-first-beginning-of-the-party-silence reigned.

"Now, what shall we play at first?" said Aunt Emmy, with overdone brightness. "Puss in the Corner?"

This suggestion was met with chilly silence.

"Hunt the Slipper?" went on Aunt Emmy, her brightness becoming almost hysterical. Silence again.

One of the guests took the matter into his own hands.

"What about a game of Hide and Seek?"

"Hide and Seek . . ." quavered Aunt Emmy. "That's rather a *rough* game, isn't it?"

They assured her that it wasn't, and drew lots for who should be "It". The Outlaws, craning necks and ears over the attic staircase, gathered that Hubert was "It".

The guests, led by Bertie Franks, swarmed upstairs in search of hiding places. They swarmed up to the first floor and the second floor and began to swarm up to the attic.

Devoid of initiative they simply followed Bertie Franks. The Outlaws withdrew hastily to their lair . . .

"Here's a little window," squeaked a

Hubert Laneite, tugging it open. "Let's go 'n' hide on the roof."

"No," said Bertie Franks earnestly. "'S dangerous. We don't want to go anywhere dangerous. We might hurt ourselves."

"And we don't want to do anythin' to get our best clothes dirty," said another Laneite.

They entered the attic opposite to the one where the Outlaws were concealed.

"We could all hide here," said a Laneite, "behind boxes and things."

"Ugh! It's rather dusty," said another Laneite with distaste.

"Never mind," said a third. "It's not for long."

"Ugh! There's spiders an' things," said a fourth disgustedly.

"Let's shut the door so's he won't see us," said Bertie Franks.

Someone shut the door and from within came sounds of the Laneites settling into hiding places, moving boxes, and uttering exclamations of disgust as they did so.

Very quietly William slipped across and turned the key in the lock. Evidently no one heard him.

"Coming!" yelled Hubert Lane from downstairs.

"Don't shout so, darling," said Aunt Emmy's flute-like voice. "Say it quietly. Little gentlemen never raise their voices."

Hubert Lane came slowly upstairs. Some instinct seemed to lead him straight up to the attic.

He stopped at the open window. His orderly mind knew that it should be shut. And it was open.

They must have gone out on to the roof.

After a moment's hesitation he squeezed out of the window and began to explore the recesses of the chimney pots.

Like a flash William, who was watching behind the door, streaked to the window, shut it and bolted it.

Hubert turned in dismay, and William had a vision of Hubert's fat pale face staring open-mouthed through the pane, before, with admirable presence of mind, he moved two large table leaves that stood near, to shut out the sight.

That disposed of Hubert.

There was no real danger. The window gave on to a stretch of flat roof, bounded by a parapet and there was no fear of the cautious Hubert venturing anywhere near it.

The Outlaws streamed out of their hiding

place to join their leader. It was evident that William had some plan.

"Come along," he said, "an' do jus' what I do."

They followed him trustfully on his bold course downstairs – right down to the hall where Aunt Emmy stood smiling painfully and pinning up her ever-descending hair.

Very faintly from upstairs from behind the barrier of window pane and table leaves there came to them an indignant, protesting "Hey!"

As to most of us hens are just hens, so to Aunt Emmy boys were just boys.

About ten boys had ascended the stairs and now about ten boys descended.

It did not occur to her that they might not be the same boys.

Even had she been less short-sighted, that possibility would not have occurred to her.

She did notice that their former spick and span appearance was somewhat blurred, but she knew that there is a powerful Law of Attraction between Boys and Dirt, and that you cannot interfere with the Laws of Nature.

She closed her eyes at the sight. Then she mastered her feelings and enquired faintly, "Where's Hubert, dears?"

William, his freckled face as expressionless as a mummy's, spoke in a mincingly polite tone of voice.

"Hubert said he was coming down in a minute and would we begin supper without him, please."

Aunt Emmy was taken aback.

She went to the bottom of the staircase. "Hubert, darling!" she called.

The real guests were still crouching behind packing cases in the attic waiting to be "found".

And Hubert's "Hey!" was too faint to reach Aunt Emmy's short hearing. The sight of the "guests" surging into the dining-room, re-called her to the scene of action.

"I think Hubert has gone to tidy himself," she said, "and I think, perhaps, you little boys should do the same."

The little boys ignored this suggestion, and, sitting down at the table, began to eat.

Aunt Emmy had always had a vague suspicion that she disliked boys, and the suspicion now grew to a certainty.

These boys refused bread and butter. They devoured iced cakes as fast as poor Aunt Emmy could hand them round. They

demanded trifle and blancmange and jelly.

They ate ravenously, as though it were some mighty task they had set themselves.

They got through enormous quantities of food.

They ate in silence, ignoring all Aunt Emmy's polite questions as to how they were getting on with their lessons at school.

They worked like Trojans. The dish of iced cakes was empty. The trifle dish was empty. The blancmange dish was empty. The cream cake dish was empty.

Only plates of plain bread and butter stood untouched.

Aunt Emmy looked at them aghast.

Louder and more indignant grew the Hubertian "Hey's!" from upstairs.

And another sound had joined them – a sound as of a pattering of many hands on a distant door.

The real guests had evidently awakened to the fact that something had gone wrong somewhere.

"Do you hear a – a – sort of *sound*?" said Aunt Emmy doubtfully, putting her hand to her ear. William looked up.

"What sort of a sound?" he demanded, fixing Aunt Emmy with his stern unblinking gaze.

"I – I think I'll go and see whatever dear Hubert's doing," said Aunt Emmy faintly, and she fled from the horrible spectacle of these ungentlemanly little boys.

William immediately opened the dining-room window, and the Outlaws, their bodies sated with the joy of the Laneite feast, their souls sated with the joy of vengeance, crept out into the night.

The Laneites had openly mocked them and spoilt their conjuring show. They had eaten the Laneites' supper.

An eye for an eye, a tooth for a tooth – a supper for a dead cat. They were quits.

Aunt Emmy found and rescued the infuriated Laneites, brought them down to the Spartan remains left them by the Outlaws,

and then went away to have a nervous break-
down quietly by herself.

Never would she have anything to do with
boys again – never, never, *never*!

Mr Lane was not in the best of tempers
when he returned home.

The vindictive cheerfulness and persistent
healthiness of his aged relative had had a very
embittering effect on him.

And the story of the Outlaws' marauding
expedition proved to be the last straw.

So he sat down at once, and wrote a

very strong letter to the Outlaws' fathers.

The fathers of the Outlaws were quite accustomed to receiving strong letters from Mr Lane. And quite often the fathers did nothing at all beyond dropping the strong letter into the wastepaper basket.

But consuming vast quantities of Lane food uninvited was a serious matter, and the heavy hand of parental retribution descended upon the Outlaws that night.

But the effect of the heavy hand is always short-lived.

The next day the Outlaws sallied out undaunted. The Laneites glowered ferociously at the Outlaws in the village street.

"Ha, ha! *You* jolly well caught it last night," said Hubert derisively.

"Hush, darling!" said William, in a shrill falsetto. "Say it quietly. Little gentlemen never raise their voices."

"I'll tell my father," said Hubert, in fury.

"Don't take any notice of them," counselled Bertie Franks. "My mother told me never to have anything to do with them."

But the Outlaws now began to rub their hands round their stomachs, smacking their lips and screwing up their faces.

"Cream cakes," said William. "Coo, *jolly* good!"

"Trifle!" murmured Ginger, rapturously.

"Jelly and blancmange," said Douglas and Henry.

This was more than even the Hubert Laneites could stand.

Unwarlike as they were, accustomed to take their stand behind Mr Lane's strong letters, they threw caution to the winds, and hurled themselves to mortal combat with the Outlaws.

It was a good fight, and revealed un-suspected resources of courage and prowess in the Hubert Laneites.

It ended in a general mix-up of Outlaws and Laneites in a muddy ditch.

There Outlaws and Laneites sat up panting

and covered with mud, and looked at each
other.

And slowly over the faces of all dawned a
grin of satisfaction.

"Go home and tell your father now," said
William to Hubert.

And Hubert, swelling with pride and joy
after his first real fight, said, "No, I won't. An'
– an' we'll fight you again," and added hastily
(for though he'd enjoyed it he'd had quite
enough for one day), "tomorrow."

Meet Just William
Richmal Crompton
Adapted by Martin Jarvis
Illustrated by Tony Ross

Just William as you've never seen him before!

A wonderful new series of *Just William* books, each containing four of his funniest stories – all specially adapted for younger readers by Martin Jarvis, the famous "voice of William" on radio and best-selling audio cassette.

Meet Just William and the long-suffering Brown family, as well as the Outlaws, Violet Elizabeth Bott and a host of other favourite characters in these ten hilarious books.

1. William's Birthday and Other Stories
2. William and the Hidden Treasure and Other Stories
3. William's Wonderful Plan and Other Stories
4. William and the Prize Cat and Other Stories
5. William's Haunted House and Other Stories
6. William's Day Off and Other Stories

Mermaid Magic
Gwyneth Rees

There's a secret world at the bottom of the sea!

Rani came to Tingle Reef when she was a baby mermaid – she was found fast asleep in a seashell, and nobody knows where she came from.

Now strange things keep happening to her – almost as if by magic. What's going on? Rani's pet sea horse, Roscoe, Octavius the octopus and a scary sea-witch help her find out . . .

The Ice-Cream Machine
Julie Bertagna

*Marshmallow Squidge, Stingy Strawberry, Chocwobble, Cheesy Peasmint –
the Potts family sells the craziest ice cream ever!*

Wayne and Wendy's parents love coming up with weird ways to make money.
But something usually goes wrong! This time they've bought an ice-cream
van called Macaroni. When Fizzbomb Sherbert gets mixed in with the ice
cream, there's chaos! The family's very naughty pet goat, Gina, is in the
middle of the trouble. And so is Macaroni, who just might be a magical
ice-cream van . . .

A funny, exciting adventure from an award-winning author.

A SELECTED LIST OF TITLES AVAILABLE
FROM MACMILLAN CHILDREN'S BOOKS